Albert Liked Ladders

First published 2005
Evans Brothers Limited
2A Portman Mansions
Chiltern Street
London W1U 6NR

British Library Cataloguing in Publication Data
Swallow, Su
        Albert liked ladders. – (Twisters)
        1. Children's stories – Pictorial works
        I. Title
        823.9'14 [J]

ISBN 0237529432
13-digit ISBN (from 1 January 2007) 9780237529437

Printed in China by WKT Company Limited

Series Editor: Nick Turpin
Design: Robert Walster
Production: Jenny Mulvanny
Series Consultant: Gill Matthews

Albert
Liked
Ladders

Su Swallow
and Barbara Nascimbeni

Evans

Albert liked ladders.

He liked ladders going up...

...and down.

But no one would let him climb their ladders.

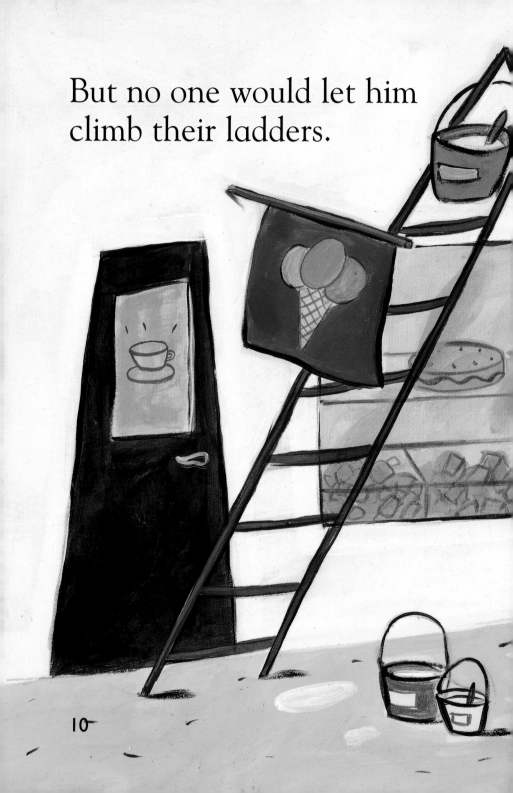

"It's too high."

13

"Too windy!"

19

20

"Too dark."

"Too slippery."

"Too old."

Albert cried.

"Follow me," said Dad.

28

"I've made a ladder just for you!"

31

Why not try reading another Twisters book?

Not-so-silly Sausage by Stella Gurney and Liz Million
ISBN 0 237 52875 4

Nick's Birthday by Jane Oliver and Silvia Raga
ISBN 0 237 52896 7

Out Went Sam by Nick Turpin and Barbara Nascimbeni
ISBN 0 237 52894 0

Yummy Scrummy by Paul Harrison and Belinda Worsley
ISBN 0 237 52876 2

Squelch! by Kay Woodward and Stefania Colnaghi
ISBN 0 237 52895 9

Sally Sails the Seas by Stella Gurney and Belinda Worsley
ISBN 0 237 52893 2

Billy on the Ball by Paul Harrison and Silvia Raga
ISBN 0 237 52926 2

Countdown by Kay Woodward and Ofra Amit
ISBN 0 237 52927 0

One Wet Welly by Gill Matthews and Belinda Worsley
ISBN 0 237 52928 9

Sand Dragon by Su Swallow and Silvia Raga
ISBN 0 237 52929 7

Cave-baby and the Mammoth by Vivian French and Lisa Williams
ISBN 0 237 52931 9

Albert Liked Ladders by Su Swallow and Barbara Nascimbeni
ISBN 0 237 52930 0